NEEL,
THE PRINCE
OF THE CLOUDS

Tania Bhattacharyya

NEEL, THE PRINCE OF THE CLOUDS
Tania Bhattacharyya

Published in 2024
© Published by

Qurate Books Pvt. Ltd.
Goa 403523,
India www.quratebooks.com
Tel: 1800-210-6527, Email: info@quratebooks.com

ISBN: 978-93-589873-9-3

"I really enjoyed the project. Your writing style gives the reader a vivid image of the imaginations. The addition of mythological references is my favourite characteristic of the story. I love your way of personification of the clouds.

Among the shayaris I liked the most, I can't narrow it down to one, but "Meri aankhen taras rahi hain" and "Akhir behaad taaluuq" are on the top."

Anubrata Bandopadhyay, "Faham"

Acknowledgements
&
Author's experience:

I am an on-line English trainer and creative artist with diverse experiences. The entire journey of writing this story has been exciting, unique and interesting. Unforeseen and enriching experiences, spontaneous flow of thoughts in new directions at different times have taken shape to give rise to this tale of hope and romance.

I never thought that a superhero will be my brainchild.   Neel-The Prince of the Clouds, the Prince coming in my dreams is very dear to me and close to my heart.

Certain unpredictable and unpleasant circumstances, long-drawn problems sometimes beyond the power of my comprehension and handling have challenged myself in many ways. This is not only with me. Societal interactions make me feel that in today's world, most of us are facing this in some way or the other in varying degrees. I feel this has subconsciously given rise to a desire of a superpower assisting me, ultimately resulting in making my creative juices flow to conceive of a superhero and feel him to the core. Imagining that the clouds that have clouded my clarity in life have also the potential to bring magic have made the process of creation really enjoyable and uplifting.

I have really felt Neel and Lina while breathing life into them.

In the course of writing the interactions between the hero and heroine and Lina's reflections, poetry stemmed from a spontaneous flow. One day I felt that a new dimension in the romance can be created if the poems are translated into Urdu. Urdu is a language that has always fascinated me.

Anubrata Bandopadhyay, a talented young artist and polyglot with whom I have recently developed acquaintance loves to write Urdu Shayaris using the pen-name ``Faham.'' Already he has published a beautiful book of Urdu poetry-"Wajoodnama." I tried to clear some understanding gaps and gain some detailed understanding from him.

I attended the program "Harf-e –Dil" ,an evening of soul-stirring ghazals and shayari by Atif Ali Khan and Aamir Ata organized on 13th April, 2024 by Kolkata Centre of Creativity to get a real feel. I loved the friendly and respectful approach towards the audience. The importance to build connection with the audience by actively involving the listeners, giving stress to assist in the understanding, repeating lines if necessary and telling the meaning of difficult words in English really impressed me.

Anubrata has translated my poems into Urdu, giving importance to the meaning and taking care to choose appropriate words. I was fascinated by the fact that Urdu words have multi-spectrum meanings. He has gone through the story, translated some Urdu portions and two Bengali poems of mine into English, and given his perspective while developing the inner meaning of the story. I felt that the inner meaning of the story should involve both a male and female perspective, so I am happy to have incorporated that.

This collaboration has been a really enjoyable experience. I feel that collaboration based on good mutual understanding generating positive vibes enhances the quality and enthusiasm of creation. This leads to flourishing of more productive creative outcomes.

My open-minded nature has made me receptive to different cultures as per my preferences. I do keep a track of both the past as well as modern advancements. So the book has diverse references to different elements of different cultures in different timelines that make it all the more interesting. My involvements with music, dance, painting and fascination for fairy tales have influenced the story.

The cover picture is my painting in mixed media and the composition has been done by me. I have sought the guidance of my mentor and eminent painter Anjan Bhattacharyya to guide me in the process and to ensure that the picture is a painting and not just an illustration. The painting has been selected in the 31st International Online Art Exhibition and Competition by Manikarnika Art Gallery from 10th July to 20th July 2024.

The back cover picture has also been done by me.

I am grateful that I live in a complex with good walking space, many trees, plants, flowers and an open ground with green grass. I can see the unfettered sky with changing shades of blue and changing forms of clouds on a regular basis. I go out for a walk regularly and enjoy every moment feeling and viewing nature. These walks have often helped to kindle my imagination and incorporate vivid imageries in this story.

I will love to dedicate this book to my parents, near and dear ones, well wishers and readers.

Introduction

Clouds have been an inseparable entity of nature, life and emotions throughout existence, time and spaces. The whole universe is a cloud in a longshot. The earth in its nascent stage had nothing but clouds. However, with time, to be habitable for life itself, clouds surrendered their toxic components and became the messenger of monsoon, the prophet of life, the avatar of revival.

Often, clouds are portrayed in different symbolic forms with varied interpretations- as message-bearer of a distant or lost lover, a romance ignitor, a boon of the heavenly, relief from the scorching summer…..or as a signal of upcoming disaster, forecast of defeat in wars, and many more.

``Neel –The Prince of the Clouds" is an eponymous fiction. The Cloud Prince, the incarnation of clouds as a beautiful hearted romantic superhero with amazing powers, is the symbol of love and hope that never dies, but changes forms. ``I change, but I cannot die".-The Cloud, P.B. Shelley

As a spectator of time and tales of different parts of the world, he beautifully connects ancient mythological elements and heritage with modern advancements. He has unmatched answers to the unanswered questions and beyond. He is poetic himself, relating to the poetries of varied languages that ever existed. He knows that magic is real, unlike we, the mortals, who ignore them or lose the endurance before the spark.

The present day woman Lina is different from the majority. The intelligence, innocence, sweetness, virtues of Lina coupled with her open-minded poetic nature sets her apart. Lina and the Cloud prince, Neel selflessly fall in love after both of them have gone through some heartbreaking episodes in their own worlds. They strike the right equation and level of mutual understanding. Their conversation through the language of poetry transcends the borders of their different worlds. They portray souls who cultivate self-love and preservation even in trying situations, steering their direction towards positivity. They have not given up hope of finding true love, even from an unexpected quarter, come what may. Lina's unquenchable curiosity and indomitable spirit gives her access to magical realism from the domain of clouds when clouds of despair had clouded her life.

Lina feels:

Beholding the monsoon clouds,

Watching the interplay of lights and shadows,

My intuition says you are here,

But where are you in the busy crowd,

All alone in an eternal wait for your true soul mate?

My eyes are deprived of your sight,

But your charisma fascinates me in my fantasy,

I can feel that you are here,

Calling my name.

I wait for you,

Lining my eyes with your dreams.

Blood rushes throughout when,

Your foot-fall strikes lightning-

I just know that you are here.

Lina is overjoyed when Neel truly comes to her-

Oh my Spring of Peace! You have come,

Into the ocean of life, my life!

I find you in the solitary blue,

I immerse into the depths of your soul,

I feel the warmth of your tender love

Caressing me like the gentle rays of the rising sun.

I see a thousand stars when I think

Of you in the darkness of sorrow.

The soothing touch of sandalwood,

Conveys me your assurance,

My wreath of love is devoted to you.

The poetry corresponds to the chants and songs for the heavenly that mankind has always done to communicate with the skies. The fantasy romantic fiction elaborates and personifies the eternal love of the mortals for the immortal with the message that there is no dearth of love for souls truly capable of loving.

The story seeks discovery of interpretations through the respective perspectives of the readers.

CONTENT

Chapter 1

Lina's Dreams   - 01

Chapter 2

Encounter with Neel, Prince of the Clouds & Romancing with the Prince   - 12

Chapter 3

Getting to Know more about Neel   - 25

Chapter 4

Neel releasing Lina from evil forces   - 31

Chapter 5

Love Forever   - 36

Chapter 1

Lina's
Dreams

Evening was approaching.

Lina was sitting in her room, humming the alaap and vistaars of some Indian classical ragas she had learnt.

Lina's eyes were beautiful and expressive. Sometimes her eyes seemed to smile, sometimes immersed in deep thought. She was fair and slender with wavy hair. Her sweetness and innocence coupled with her firmness and intelligence contributed to her interesting features.

She loved the slow paced soulful alaaps very much immersing her in deep feelings. She had the habit of listening to compact instrumental recitals, mostly flute recitals of different ragas in a soothing volume– the effect was heavenly. The way the patterns of the raga unfolded and flowed in myriad ways awakened the sea of her emotions, generating waves of different dimensions, waterfalls cascading down her nervous system as relieving and refreshing cool currents of chills. Often she felt like dancing, reacting spontaneously. The recitals were the perfect accompaniment during her daily meditation regime.

Today the tranquility generated by the raga Kirmani, a very romantic raga made her fall asleep for a short while. During her short spell of slumber she had a beautiful dream.

She saw that she was dancing alone in her room. The freedom of the movements was giving her a sense of liberty from the thorns of her life.

While dancing when she came to her verandah she saw a beautiful cloud in such close proximity! It was a white fleecy cloud of such beautiful shape floating in front of her at an arm's distance! She instinctively felt a desire to touch it. The moment she touched it with her delicate finger and felt the softness…. a magic happened. She found herself sitting on the cloud and flying.

She screamed but the cloud would not stop. She was afraid if she fell down. But she felt soft hands caressing and holding her from all directions. The cloud had extended projection from its various corners shielding her comfortably. She was firmly anchored to her seat. Very soon her uneasiness went away and she literally started enjoying. She lay down on the cloud. How soft the surface was, how stable she felt! She had a very pleasant sensation in her head. She felt her troubles sinking and her head getting lighter as a feather.

She felt ecstatic and clapped her hands in joy. She seemed to be on cloud nine!

The rumbling of clouds awakened her from her spell of slumber. She awoke from her stupor. She was disappointed that she was lying on her bed and not on a cloud. But somehow the clouds outside beckoned her. She went to the verandah and saw the cloudy cover of the sky. It was raining.

After that her mind was preoccupied with clouds. Only if her dream came true!

....

....

Next morning she woke up early. A pleasant cloudy morning greeted her. Her daily routine started on a pleasurable note. She noticed her feelings were different. Some unknown joy was invigorating her. She was humming some of her favorite romantic songs.

She went out in the afternoon for a walk. The sun had come up. She noticed some unusual happenings. In front of her a long stretch of the path was lit up by the sun. But when she stepped, suddenly the sun went away and a pleasant shade cast itself over the entire path. The moment she had completed walking she looked behind. To her surprise the path was sunlit like before.

The same thing happened in other areas also while she walked. She came back home, quite bewildered. She could not easily dismiss what she had experienced.

The next day it was raining very hard and she had to go out. A gusty wind was also blowing. She was shivering and feeling uncomfortable. But a magic happened. The moment she stepped outdoors, the rain stopped, the wind became agreeable in nature. She felt relieved and happily started on her journey. Such uniform weather conditions prevailed throughout her stay outside. Her mind was also filled with very positive and joyous thoughts. Her inner thoughts reflected on her face and eyes, and her cheeks appeared rosier than usual. She was very gay and while she walked she felt buoyant and light as a feather, as if she was floating, gliding her way smoothly like a graceful dancer.

That night her eyelids drooped with sleep. She slept soundly and had a beautiful dream. She was flying on a cloud in the night sky. All the stars appeared like glittering diamonds. A blue bird was sitting on one corner of the half moon. White night flowers started blooming all around caressing the moon when she arrived in close proximity. The gentle night breeze became loaded with the beautiful fragrance of the garland of flowers. She felt someone holding her hand, assisting her to alight on the moon. She sat on the moon and felt very sleepy. She kissed the moon and fell asleep. The wind gently played with her long soft tresses. For a long time she had not experienced such deep sound sleep.

....

....

She woke up when the night was melting into dawn. The dream was so real that she felt she was truly sleeping on the moon but to her disappointment she found herself lying on her bed. She loved her bed. She felt it is not proper to give gratitude to God to have a nice bed to sleep. Only she wanted the dream to be real.

She drew open the curtain beside her bed and gazed at the sky. The waning crescent-shaped moon was visible. The moon was almost alike the moon in her dreams. She felt maybe she was on the moon all this while and the cloud had transported her to bed just a few minutes ago.

Why was she dreaming of a cloud?

Life was now like a mirage. Some roadblocks seemed to be irremovable, however she tried; she tried to extricate herself but she stumbled-she did not create any trouble, but troubles surmounted –she had to create her own oasis.

But this situation was thrilling also. She was learning to handle herself better in difficult and uncertain situations. But sometimes certain things crossed a limit which bewildered her. Again she had to find out a way to secure a foothold.

A drought had been created in her soul. Her eyes often mirrored her internal thirst - thirst for peace and love.

She was a bit poetic by nature, and had a fondness for Urdu shayaris. She had an eclectic choice and she liked the Urdu language because it was one of the most sophisticated languages, defining beauty and grace. So when she thought or spoke poetically, she would often translate her thoughts in Urdu.

My eyes are thirsty, there is thirst throughout my soul.............

My imagination flies to some distant abode........................

Meri ankhen taras rahi hain, mere ruh ko qarar nahi...

Tasavvur me hai ek manzil ba'iid...

Note: The Urdu translations have been done by poet with pen-name "Faham." Urdu words have a wide spectrum of meanings, but for the convenience of understanding, I am giving the meanings as per what I have meant in the context of the story. Readers are free to make their own interpretations.

Ruh-soul,spirit

Qarar-peace

Tasavvur-imagination

Ba'iid-distant,remote

Somehow for the last few days the cloud was raining love in the deepest recesses of her heart generating ripples of peace. She had developed such a fondness for the cloud! The cloud seemed so dear to her, such an inseparable part of her existence! The cloud seemed to be a harbinger of a new foundation in her life.

....

....

She looked at the sky often. Her eyes were searching for the cloud she had seen in her dreams. The cloud of her dreams-had it followed her when she had gone out? Did she have an invisible lover residing on that cloud who had fallen in love with her?

She had read the great poet Michael Madhusudan Dutt's magnum opus Meghnad Badh Kavya few years ago. She felt as if she was Promila and she had a lover like Indrajit who was there atop in his celestial chariot, playing hide and seek with her amidst the clouds. Just as he was an expert in illusion warfare techniques, maybe his love making also had the touches of illusion. Indrajit had celestial weapons and was very well versed in magic. The character of Promila was created by Dutt inspired by warrior princesses Clorinda, Camilla from western epics who had their tribe of female warriors. Somehow, she had admired the courage, beauty and devotion of Promila. Only she disliked the tragic ending where she self-immolated herself following the death of her dear husband. In some texts Indrajit's wife is referred to as Sulochona. Indrajit had defeated Indra so she felt that when she had walked, applying his mastery over magic he had combated Indra's airavat to stop the heavy rains for the sake of his lover. Maybe the cloud was from Indraloka.

Or was this cloud a messenger of love? Was a lover from faraway lands trying to convey his love to her through the Cloud Messenger as in Kalidas's Megahdoota?

I search for you, Oh Cloud!

When would you come again?

Come to me, come to me…………

And make me fly yet again………..

Making me sit on your lap………………

Take me to the moon again

Take me, take me……………………….

Ay Baadal! main tumhe dhundhti hun,

Phir kab aoge?

Ao mere pas, udkar le chalo mujhe,

Bithakar teri agosh me, le chalo mujhe,

Chand ki or, udkar le chalo mujhe…

Agosh-lap

…………………………………………………………………………………

………………………………………………………………………………..

That   night she had a dream………………………………………..

Her favourite cloud was visible, but this time on the cloud she saw a princely man in ornaments and royal clothes…………………………………he was practicing the graceful, powerful movements of the Tai-Chi martial arts form with such elegance…………a beautiful spirituality was being emanated from him and she could hear Chinese melody flowing in the background…………………………………this practice was interspersed with soulful dance assuming Indian sculpturesque poses in his own style and mood in tune with beautiful soulful flute renditions of Indian ragas-Bhairavi, Khambaj……………………… she was spellbound…

He was wearing a silver diamond-studded turban and beautifully draped white dhoti of rich silk………….a silver flowing cloak and a royal blue top………….. silver and diamond ornaments……….a beautiful silver belt clasped his slender waist……….a pair of silver nagra adorned his feet…………..

She had never seen such a graceful handsome man! His facial expressions mirrored a beautiful heart.

His face had a dreamy, soft, pleasant expression that instantly struck a chord with her……………….

Suddenly he developed a pair of white beautiful wings, swooped down and came up to her……………he stood in front of her hovering with his right hand extended as if asking her hand…………………..

She exclaimed and woke up……………..she was on her bed……………..she went outside and saw the night sky but could not see the cloud and the lover in her dreams……………………

…………………………………………………………………………………………

…………………………………………………………………………………………..

The next night in her dream he appeared in one of his Western avatars in a white shirt with the upper part a bit unbuttoned, black pants complementing his beautiful legs with a beautiful golden belt hugging his waist. He was wearing beautiful black shoes. What a swag and style he had! He was dancing on the cloud using beautiful manly and graceful Western movements with Western romantic musical accompaniment. Then he suddenly grew a pair of wings and flew towards the full moon. He landed on the moon and his wings disappeared. He started moon-walking with such grace and ease!

In her sleep she was admiring him like anything! She noticed that he stopped dancing and took out a glittering diamond necklace from one of the pockets in his pant. He seemed to smile at her and from his hand threw the necklace downwards. The necklace descended down the night sky and then she saw her standing outside in the dark in a beautiful garden. The necklace comfortably slipped down her head and settled on her neck. She was surprised. She looked up and she saw him. Then again she could not see him, but then again saw him peeping from behind the clouds. He played hide and seek with her from the sky for a while. She was so engrossed in seeing him, then searching for him…….then he waved and disappeared.

She woke up. When she opened her eyes, she was amazed to see the same necklace just beside her pillow. She did not know what to say. She wore it and went outside in the verandah. She looked up and saw nobody. She came back and stood in front of her mirror. The dazzling diamonds in the necklace were shining in the moonlight and she looked amazing!

She did not want to take off the necklace, but she certainly could not wear it in daytime in front of others. The necklace had to be a secret hidden from the eyes of others. She carefully opened her almirah and kept the necklace in a bag inside her locker before the break of dawn.

....
....

The next night he again appeared in her dreams.

He was wearing a beautiful silvery white suit and pant.

He spoke. She heard his manly voice for the very first time.

"I am Neel, Prince of the Clouds. I saw you one day as I was travelling on a cloud and fell in love with you."

She dreamt herself atop on his cloud, standing in close proximity to him in a white flowing gown.

"Today I will show you my vahanas and astras. I never hurt or injure anybody in any fight. My tactics are quite different. I mainly employ illusion warfare techniques."

He whistled, and with each whistle a magical celestial weapon or a vahana/vehicle made a special appearance in front of her as follows-

Modern versions of the following weapons that had been gifted to him by different Gods-

Vayvayastra-generating powerful winds

Suryaastra-generating dazzling rays of light

Varunastra-creating torrential waves of water

Sammohana-making people collapse in a trance

Bhoumastra-creates deep underground tunnels

Parjanyastra-creates thunder clouds

Parvatastra-making mountains fall from the sky

Nagapasha-helping to bind target in snakes

Antardhana Astra-makes something or someone disappear

Prajnastra-restores senses

Sailastra-makes all winds vanish

He had the following vehicles and vahanas(animal consorts)-

A magnificent peacock chariot

A white unicorn with wings able to fly and run on the sky, on water and land

A glamorous, tough awesome car of bluish silver colour-one of the most advanced 5th generation cars with self-charging hybrid electric technology, muscular stance, refined stature, good degree of safety, power-backed acceleration, higher fuel efficiency

A Luxury Car of Saphhire Blue colour meant for cruising the sky in a relaxed mood

The cars could fly in the air, if required could be driven on land and also transform into hi-tech submarines in water.

She was awestruck and about to ask him something, but he vanished.

She woke up and saw nobody but a beautiful peacock feather was there on her bed beside her pillow.

....

....

❖ ❖ ❖

Chapter 2

Encounter with Neel, Prince of the Clouds & Romancing with the Prince

She was feeling like talking to the Prince of the Clouds, but she was checking herself.

I am so thirsty to get a glimpse of you, want to talk with you

……..

But I also have the fear,

In this age there is scarcity of love,

And rain also does not have life in the desert…………

If close affinity can also be the reason of disunion….

I feel that if I can still hold my breath,

It is necessary to maintain distance.

Apki ek jhalak ko mera waqt tarasta hai, baat karne ka man hota hai…

Magar ye bhi dar hai, is zamane me pyar ki qillat hai, aur sahra me barish ki koi zindagi nahin…

Akhir behad talluuq hi to furqat ki bhi wajah hai…

Kahin lagta hai,

agar sanson me rukawat na aye to

fasila rakhna wajib hai.

Qillat-scarcity

Sahra-desert

Talluuq-relation, affinity

Furqat-Disunion

Fasila-Some distance

Wajib-necessary

Suddenly she saw the Prince of the Clouds standing in front of her in her room, echoing every single line she was thinking to her amazement.

She asked, "How do you read my mind?"

"Because I love you."

"Why do you love me?"

She noticed Neel's eyes glistening with tears.

He started. His voice seemed to emerge from a heavy heart. He also loved Urdu shayaris.

Happiness is a moment in the epoch of sorrow…

Solitude always stays a bit longer…

Pal bhar ki khushi sadiyon ka malal hai…… … … … …

Tanhai hamesha thoda zyada hai…… … … …..

He paused.

She looked at him questioningly.

"Why are you so lonely? Why are you so sad?"

He replied, "Now I am not lonely. Now I am not sad. You are the light of my life. ''

He looked at her endearingly.

" I know certain unreasonable problems, demands and denials are troubling you. Do not worry. I know you need help. I have come to help you, to love you, to assure you, to comfort you, to give the power to surmount the obstacles in your life, and to make you feel that a man loves you ,considers you reasonable and does not like others troubling you in different ways."

"Why do you love me?"

She reiterated the question.

Then she continued,

"For the last few years, I have thought that the little boat of my precious life after wading through many waters will settle at the shore. My direction is, and has always been towards light. But the light towards which I have sailed has often been like a flickering flame.

Unexpectedly clouds have come in, clouding my vision and clarity.

Then I have felt often like a cloud drifting aimlessly, indifferent to wordly affairs. Again I had vowed to see the silver lining, ...light wispy happy clouds, clouds bathed in the different shades of sunrise and sunset, the rays of sun peeping through clouds ....and travel, and yet another cloud of despair and confusion from an unexpected angle............but the sacred flame of love, faith and belief in God and life has been, and is still alive. Going upstream again and again, giving gratitude to God for every little good thing I have got has been and will be my ritual. But sometimes it is exhausting, even to hope when the same unreasonable problems go on being repeated despite the best of efforts to put an end. Nowadays I feel many things are so unreasonable, the extent of many things spiraling out of control creating strange problems. Amidst all this I make efforts to lead myself properly, but now I am a bit exhausted.

There is a lot to see and explore in this world created by God but conscious efforts need to be done to shift the mindset and perspective to experience peace, happiness and beauty which was earlier not required. I have decided to lead a beautiful life, but still cannot help but think sometimes-

In the world perpetually changing colours,

In the world changing facts according to needs,

However true looks the possibility of loving,

The changing faces create the situation of fear,

Who is up to what...

Har pal apna rang badalti hui duniya me,

Zarurat ke mutabiq dhalti hui duniya me,

Mohabbat chahe jitna bhi mumkin lage

Badalte in chehron ki mashaqqat yahi hai-

Ghabrahat hoti hai

Itne Naqabon me kiska kya irada hai.

Mashaqqat-trouble,pain

Naqab-masked

Then she paused, looked at Neel, and continued-

Feelings are at odds with experience,

Light is prismatic by passing through clouds.

Fir bhi ehsas ki tajurbe se bagawat hai,

Badlon se hokar hi aaj nuur ki nusrat hai.

Tajurbe-experience

Bagawat-revolt

Neel smiled assuringly, "Clouds have clouded your vision and clarity. Now from the abode of clouds someone special has come to love you and give you light."

Lina felt so blessed.

Neel said, "I will come again. Do not worry. You will get all your answers."

He flew away. Today he was in a sky blue glittery outfit. Today it was not a dream, but a real encounter. When she looked at the sky, the sky seemed to glitter with diamonds.

....

....

She went out in the verandah in dawn. She stretched her arms upwards. She was feeling very happy.

Suddenly she found herself flying on a cloud with the Prince of the Clouds seated beside her. He was wearing a pristine white suit with mirrors reflecting light in different directions. She was not dreaming. She winked her eyes, pinched herself – yes, she was not dreaming. He touched her with a magic silver wand and to her amazement she was wearing a beautiful dress with beautiful satin roses stitched on it. Surprisingly, for the last few days she was dreaming of a dress with roses, and now she was wearing one. She was amazed.

Suddenly she started crying. Tears trickled down her cheeks and the tear droplets fell on the cloud. She noticed that her tears made beautiful flowers bloom.

The Prince was looking at her thoughtfully with genuine concern. He came closer, clasped her and drew her towards his bosom.

She had a heavenly feeling. Her mind of late was full of contradictions and confusing thoughts. She was not finding any direction in certain areas in her life. She was feeling that however sincerely she tried she always met with some unprecedented obstacle. The love and kindness that she showered on others was not always repaid in the proper way. Her requirements were not given due importance at times. She did have deep unwavering faith in God, but of late she was struggling to keep herself calm and collected.

But when locked in embrace with the Prince, she felt all her confusions melting away, and her brain immersing in the waters of the fountains of ethereal love.

Two hearts truly in love do not need words to speak. Silence speaks volumes. The cloud was floating in the blue eternity. The surrounding serenity created such an ambient atmosphere for lovemaking!

Time passed by.

The Prince of the Clouds broke the silence.

" Smile, smile my dear."

Very affectionately he wiped away her tears and caressed her cheeks.

She smiled.

The Prince said, "Now I will show you some magic."

Her face instantly lighted up in a bright smile.

"Ready?" he asked .

"Sure, why not?" she replied. Her voice was so lively.

The Prince started whirling around her. When he whirled, his full form was not at all discernable. He seemed to be like a blue ball of wind.

Suddenly he disappeared. For a long time she could not see him. Then suddenly he came and stood in front of her. She was startled, but at the same time burst into laughter. Then he started to whirl again. She stood wondering looking here and there.

He got stationed at a different point. He kicked a small wisp of cloud like a football. The cloud rose upwards and got amplified into seven clouds, bathed in the seven colours of the rainbow. Then he whistled, and she saw a rainbow connecting the seven clouds. She clapped like a child happily.

She wished if she could wear a rainbow coloured beautiful gown. No sooner had she thought, she felt the Prince near her touching her dress with a magic wand……….and yes, she was wearing such a beautiful rainbow coloured dress! She suddenly felt herself flying on a cloud with the Prince and there she was standing on the green coloured cloud, the cloud in the middle of the VIBGYOR sequence. The Prince flew down and whistled. She saw him holding a camera. He stood steadily on a big cloud and took her photographs, while the cloud on which she was standing had developed projections, creating a protective boundary around her.

Suddenly she saw him holding an odhni of the seven shades of the rainbow and his outfit transformed into a fantastic rainbow coloured top and rainbow coloured pants with a silver belt bordered by golden rims on both sides hugging his slender waist. He very stylishly flung the odhni towards her. She was surprised how effortlessly her hand attracted the odhni. She started to dance joyfully on the cloud with the odhni! She had never danced on a cloud! She never felt unstable or she would fall down, but so stable and light! The Prince also came and joined her in the dance of love and ecstasy.

The Prince said, "I have been seeing you for a long time from the top of the clouds when you go out for a walk."

She exclaimed, "That is why I feel so much loved when I go out for my walks. I have often felt that I am being showered with love by some secret lover, but never thought this to be true."

A series of golden hued fleecy clouds lined parallely in a series appeared. She was spellbound, admiring the beauty.

The Prince looked into her eyes and said,

"Maybe you are faced by complications from humans in the earth. You feel they are so complex, unreasonable, troublesome, confusing, irritating with peculiar social conceptions and annoying generalized notions! There may be some troublesome position of planets or troubles created by people who do not work on themselves or update themselves to lead themselves in an improved way! But that does not mean there is no love. You see God has created every creation with a purpose, and to make every creation of his feel loved. People do not value his creations or the virtues he gives. They cannot even mostly tolerate the virtues in others. They go on wrecking themselves and others but you are not like that. So why will you feel deprived of love? If you have faith in life, you give gratitude to God, you must have the belief that you will find love in some quarter."

She felt so soothed by the words. She replied, " I always make efforts to lead myself in a better way and restore my belief in the goodness of life, the hope of finding love. I give gratitude to God for all I have got, am getting and ask pardon if I am having bad experiences and tell me to help me and give strength. "

He said softly," I appreciate that."

She was surprised. "Really? Yes, few appreciate, many do not."

He said, "So those people make up the whole world? Those horrible people! Kick them out of your life and mind as far as possible and kick-start a new phase of love with me."

She replied, "I can and have kicked out many, but few I cannot. That is where the concern lies."

Neel said, "For the time being don't even think of them. I will help you."

He smiled in an assuring way, " I love you just the way you are."

He smiled, "You want me to sing for you?"

She smiled and blushed.

Suddenly a piano descended from the sky and landed gently on a cloud with a stool. He sat on the stool and started singing, looking at her with his beautiful in-depth expressions. He had such a lovely manly romantic voice!

I have seen many stars, but not any star shining as brightly as your eyes,

I have seen the petals of flowers, but not any petal as soft and delicate as your lips……….

I have seen many lights, but not the radiance generated by your smile……

I have seen many angels flying amidst the clouds, but not any angel with your angelic grace………………

In the vicinity of many beauties there has been much distance in the closeness…………..

I feel close with you even when you are at a distance……………

I can feel you deeply even when there is blissful silence...............

Dekha hai maine sitare hazaron,

Yun damakta dekha nahin

Magar teri ankhon jaisi.

Dekha hai maine gul hazaron,

Yun nazuk dekha nahin

Magar teri labon jaisi.

Dekha hai maine ziya hazaron,

Yun chamakta dekha nahin

Magar teri muskarahat jaisi.

Dekha hai maine farishte hazaron,

Yun malkuti dekha nahin

Magar teri shokhi jaisi.

Duri mehsus hui husn ke paas baithkar bhi,

Mai tujhse dur na hua tujhse dur hokar bhi.

Andheron me bhi tera nur dikhta hai,

Sannaton me bhi milti hai teri awaz,

Meri har lagan hai muntazir Teri hi,

Tujhpe qurban hai meri har ehsas.

Sannaton-silence

Muntazir-expectant, one who waits

They were having a whale of a time.

Suddenly she saw many white horses with wings and unicorns, their hoofs being replaced by paintbrushes. They immersed their hoofs in ponds of different colours and the droplets splashed on a big white paper lying on a big cloud. The colours flowed, mixed and created myriad beautiful patterns.

Then the horses came closer to the paper and with deft strokes, painted a dream scene of lovemaking of the Prince of the Clouds with her. After the painting was done, the painting suddenly flew from the cloud and became straight, as if displaying itself. She was mesmerized.

She sat gazing at the painting.

The Prince of the Clouds said, " Not today, but another day I will make you paint sitting on the clouds. ''

She was so excited! "When, when?"

Neel replied, "Within a few days…………..Now I will drop you to your home.."

She did not want to leave Neel.

"Why do you love me?" she asked.

Neel :

"You still ask me why I love you-

I also do not know the exact reason

What happened to me when I saw you walking while I was travelling on a cloud…………..

I cannot explain

But I could not forget you.

I felt like the fountain of love like a rainbow

Had appeared after many clouds had enveloped me…..

Out of the cloudy state of confusion I seem to rise

When I behold the light in your eyes

When I behold the light in your eyes

Believes Neel, the Prince of the Clouds,

The light will always shine.

Ab bhi sawal karti ho mujhe tumse muhabbat qyun hai?

Kash ye mujhe bhi ilm hota…

Magar mai baadlon me safar karte hue tujhe dekhne ka zikr kar sakta hun,

pata nahi us nazar ka kya asar hua,

magar shayd us asar me ye aj ka alam shamil hai.

Us mulaqat k bad tum mere har waqt me rahe, shokh si chamki,

kabhi jharne si bahi, magar har waqt bas tu hi tu rahi.

Shahzad-e-Baadal par hi baadal sa chha gayi, maine ankhen band ki aur fir tu hi aa gayi.

Ye teri ankhon me jab nuur dekhta hun

Ye teri ankhon me jab nuur dekhta hun

Yakin hai mujhe Shahzad-e-baadal Neel,

ye nuur jahan me raushan rahegi,

meri jahan, tu raushan rahegi.

Ilm-knowledge

Zikr-remembrance

Shokh-bright as colour

Nuur-light

Neel smiled, " I will come again, don't worry. More magic is waiting for you."

A cloud came to her. She sat on the cloud, and the cloud carried her to home.

She felt that she had two homes now-her home and her new home in the abode of the clouds.

. . . .

. . . .

❖ ❖ ❖

Chapter 3

Getting to Know
more about Neel

One day she went out in the afternoon. In the summer the heat had eased a bit. She went and sat beside a lake under the shady cover of trees. A light breeze was blowing creating beautiful ripples in the pond. The ripples were generated in the centre and gradually spread towards the periphery.

Near the bank there were rotund lotus leaves, full and half-blown lotus flowers- pink, fresh, delicate. She loved lotus flowers. But she observed something. In the peripheral space occupied by the lotus flowers and leaves the water was relatively still.

The breeze was reviving, and she heard a train moving in the distance.

The sunlight and shade swam over her creating trembling irregular patches. The summer breeze stirred the water and the trees but not the lotus bank.

Of course the lotus bank must have been experiencing the indirect effects of the breeze and ripples but maybe was oblivious, unconscious. Maybe the visible manifestation was not there though the feelings were there deep inside.

The sky was dotted with wispy clouds. It was a rare sight to see fresh lotus flowers in bloom in such heat.

Why was Neel sad? What was his history?

Lina was wondering.

She wondered and wondered………….

Suddenly she saw a cloud with the Prince of the Clouds atop, beckoning her. He held her hand, and she found herself sitting on the cloud beside him, flying over a very beautiful blue lake with waters as clear as crystal.

Neel started to give an account of his past life.

"I am the son of the Queen of the Sea and the King of the Moon.

When I grew up he fell in love with Rupali, a beautiful lady in the abode of the moon. But just as the moon has spots, Rupali was not spotless in her character. She flirted with me. She tried to use my supernatural powers for her own selfish benefits and later fell for the Prince of the Sea.

I was heartbroken. Yet, I had not given up hope of finding true love.

I have many supernatural abilities. I will put them to use to help you. I know you will not ask for it, but I feel it is God's wish to make me come to you and be by your side. ''

"Can I meet your parents?"

" Actually they will not like if I love a daughter of Mother Earth, they think too highly of themselves. I do not want you to face their wrath.

But that does not stop me from loving you, coming to you or protecting you.

I also want to tell you something. You should not disclose to anyone you know about my existence in your life. You know that you have me by your side. It is not that I am not transparent and want to hide, but I am not meant to mix with mortal human beings. Mortal human beings may cause danger to me if they know my existence. You just know."

Lina trusted Neel more than she could trust any human being except her mother. Lina nodded her head in assent.

Neel said, "I will always be yours, that I can assure. I will always come to you. Only you will be able to see me."

Neel told her to close her eyes.

He kissed her eyelids thrice.

Lina felt all anxiety, worries, apprehensions melting away.

Neel whistled and his unicorn arrived.

Neel said, "Now sit by my side and see the beauty the world has to offer from different corners."

The unicorn spread out its long wings, flew over the sky, ran over the clouds and sometimes sped over the waters, soil and grass.

The clouds drifted, and Lina saw-

The most beautiful of gardens, flowers in bloom, luscious fruits-

The most beautiful of ponds and waterfalls, lakes and oceans,

The most beautiful of birds and animals-

The most sacred places of worship

The most humble, strong and beautiful hearts

The sweetest of fairies and angels-

Sweet babies blossoming and smiling

Laughing and playing

In the cradle of nature.

Jo baadal hate,

Lina ke ain hue sabse haseen wadiyan,

jinme bahaar mubaraq phool khile the,

sabse umda aur lazeez mewe,

jannati jamaal talaab,

jharne, jheel aur samandaron ki angdaiyan.

Ithlate parinde,

balkhati zindagi,

aur sabse paak ibadatkhane.

Itne shant, durust aur mast dil, farishte, aur utne hi mithe nau-zaid, khilte aur muskarate chehre

qudrat ki agosh me.

Neel smiled, "See, I will make you paint today in a way you have never painted before."

Paintbrushes and colours came to her flying on a cloud. Neel handed her with a paintbrush and said, "Dip the brush in any colour you like."

She dipped the brush in vibrant yellow colour.

Neel smiled excitedly, "Now hold my hand."

Holding Lina's hand, he made the yellow droplets of the brush splash on a beautiful white fleecy cloud. The colour created beautiful patterns. Lina stared in amazement.

Similarly she dipped her brush in other colours playfully like a child and holding Neel's hands splashed the colour droplets. She had never dreamt she would paint a cloud, that too so beautifully. At the end the cloud with all the lovely patterns looked ethereal.

Lina sat with Neel on a cloud leaning her head on Neel's shoulder. Both of them sat enjoying the view of the cloud and the warmth of their breath.

She saw little unicorns emerging from the clouds carrying sweet little babies. Lina loved babies very much. The unicorns alighted on the cloud they were sitting on and gently placed the babies on the cloud. Lina had a lovely time playing, hugging and kissing the babies accompanied by Neel.

....
....

Lina felt, life is not like mathematics. All equations do not match with the proper solution and out of that problems and situations come up that seem so strange. But still if one has faith in strength of mind and love, then one can also experience the surprises life has to offer, the surprising turn of events that make life exciting as well.

If clouds had not clouded her life, she would not have experienced the surprise and magic possible by clouds. The river of life would have flowed in the same way, in the same pace. Due to unexpected change in direction, new tributaries would not have been created. There would have been no thrill. Opportunities would not have been created to view people from different walks of life. Thoughts would not have developed to view life from multiple perspectives.

It is not always fun to experience this. It is not always easy to go through this. There is every chance to lose direction, becoming hopeless to find a proper direction. The proper direction may take time to come and the patience and faith in life may go away. But this in itself is a test. The test is to hold on to hope, patience, giving gratitude and strong belief in the goodness life is offering and has in reserve. Leading oneself properly, looking after oneself and cultivating self-love during such a time is very important. Then only one's soul gets elevated to experience the miracles of life and understand higher thoughts and greater truths.

Neel was not always by her side in the visible world, but in her inner world she always felt him. She felt, there are many ladies who hold hands of a tangible companion but have superficial feeling of attachment.

But for her, Neel had embraced her whole being to generate the positive feelings of peace, happiness, love, calmness, assurance empowering her with a certain divine strength she had never sensed before. When Neel was not with her, she could very well see him in her mind's eye. Envisioning him would give her a powerful feeling of strength and security, as if he was imparting his power to her.

She did have certain people in her life always standing beside her through thick and thin, but of late some forces have been acting to pull her down and she was giving the effort against the tide so that she was not. The same forces have once pulled her up, but these forces were sometimes pulling her up, and pulling her down.

Neel was God-sent in her life. Mutually they derived strength from each other and tried to dispel the darkness of the clouds surrounding them from time to time.

. . . .
. . . .

Chapter 4

Neel releasing Lina
from evil forces

Neel told her, "For the next few days there will be grey clouds, rain and storm as per God's wish. You stay safe and sound. Close your eyes. You will be able to see me whenever you wish. I will also do something magical for you."

Lina was thrilled.

The next morning she woke up and was greeted by gusty winds and rumbling of clouds. She closed her eyes and had one fantastic vision after the other.

She saw Neel in a different avatar-dark and divine, rebellious and determined, his sharp observant yet pleasant eyes mirroring steady resolve and steely determination. His hair- long, black and thick with beautiful wavy texture like the tresses of Lord Shiva had spread across the sky. As per the saying "Like repels like", it seemed that his darkness was meant to repel darkness. Neel was initially floating on a cloud but he visualized two forces of obstacle coming towards him-a ghastly black and the other a blackish blue demon-like being, fearful to behold.

He whistled and got hold of the Parvatastra. A big blue mountain fell from the sky and landed in front of the black and blue forces, blocking their way.

Neel stood on the peak of the mountain with poise and firmness. He looked like a valiant warrior, at the same time so divine!

The blue and black forces got startled but did not give up. They tried to climb up the mountain as they could not find any way out. But the more they tried, the mountain became bigger and bigger.

Huffing and puffing, however they struggled, they did not give up.

Neel smiled and to trick their senses, suddenly made the mountain very short. They were delighted to reach the peak and see Neel. But suddenly Neel disappeared with the help of the Antardhana Astra. They got baffled. Try as they might, however they ran, craned their neck, in whatever direction they looked, they could not find any trace of Neel.

Suddenly they found themselves being lifted into the sky by a whirl of wind. They started screaming. At one point the whirl of wind did not make them fly up further, but instead made them whirl and whirl. They were not falling down, they were screaming, their head churned- sometimes the whirling was clockwise, sometimes anti-clockwise.

Neel had applied the Vayvayastra to generate the winds and from a distance was watching with a mischievous smile on his face. He did give a tough time to his opponents, but he never hurt or injured anyone.

Actually, these were the two forces that were clouding Lina's life. Neel, the Prince of the Clouds was now fighting to paralyze these two hindering forces. Lina had the strength to do the best in the worst of situations created by the forces, not giving up her faith and goodness. But she did not have the ability to paralyze the forces. God had been kind enough to answer Lina's sincere prayers for help. God had been satisfied with the gratitude Lina had constantly given for all the goodness she had received, how Lina had constantly asked for pardon of any sin that was responsible for her suffering and sent the Prince of the Clouds to fight the forces so that Lina can have a better life.

Something happened beyond Neel's expectation. The dark forces, assembling all their strength stopped the whirling. The speed of whirling became slow. Neel gave more power to his Vayvayastra but still the dark forces were able to diminish the speed of rotation. Of course Neel expected resistance and challenge from the opponents and was ready to tackle unexpected situations.

He used the Sammohana astra. The forces collapsed in a trance and became still.

But how long will the spell of Sammohana astra will last on them was a question.

Neel used Bhoumastra to create a deep underground tunnel near the base of the mountain. With the help of the Nagapasha the two forces were bound so strongly by the snakes that there was no path of escape. In Neel's peacock chariot descended the two dark forces. Then Neel directed the snakes and the peacock to place the two forces near the deep tunnel. The forces were released with the spell of Sammohana astra still operative. With the help of Varunastra, torrential waves of water were generated that carried the two forces deep into the tunnel. Neel sealed the mouth of the tunnel with soil. Then he made a mountain descend on the whole tunnel ensuring there was no way to go out from the upper side.

At least the dark forces were made captive for the time being. But the forces were in a trance and Neel had to make out how long the spell will last.

Hours passed, and everything remained still. Neel, being vigilant, took some rest.

Lina also experienced an inner calm and decrease of turbulence in her emotions by disturbances. There was stillness along with darkness.

All of a sudden there was a trembling……………..the intensity of the trembling increased. Neel became alert. The evil forces were coming out of the trance but were not being able to come out of the tunnel. The weight of the mountain above was very heavy. The walls of the tunnel were very firm and thick, the mouth was very firmly sealed.

Only the trembling went on for some time, but nothing else. The trap that Neel had set was very difficult to break.

It could not be broken in the long run.

....

....

Lina genuinely sensed that she was released from some uneasy forces that had kept her captive for a long time. She saw the Prince of the Clouds standing in front of her, his face beaming with delight.

"Want to go for a long drive?"

Lina: "Why not?"

Neel whistled and two cars came flying.

"On which car?" Neel asked.

Lina: "Both."

Neel said, "Sure, why not! We will alternate."

The doors of one car opened automatically. The cloud on which Lina was sitting went near the car. Lina entered and sat ……the feeling was great! Neel sat beside her and got hold of the steering. What a wonderful feeling it was when the car started moving in the sky! To her amazement she saw the other car following them. She wondered how can the other car move without a driver and be self-steered! But in the abode of clouds, so many impossible things were possible by magic!

Suddenly Neel held her hand, she flew with him and sat in the other car. Then Neel started driving, the other car started following them.

The joy-ride on the sky was an unbelievably amazing experience for Lina!

How she wished her permanent destination was in the clouds with her dearest Neel!

Chapter 5

Love
Forever

When Neel came to her, he actually made her invisible to mortal eyes. He was also invisible. He kept on coming to her-making her fly when there was a huge traffic jam, taking her to her favourite destinations over a cloud or his cars, peacock chariots, unicorns; making troublesome people talking or behaving with her unfavorably fall in a trance . Once it so happened that one lady whom she hated the most started blurting out, she started flying in a ball of wind and scream as she might she could not descend – Lina laughed and clapped happily.

Whenever she was in need or had a problem she would call Neel and he would give importance to her like none other. He would always find or try to find some innovative solution and make her spellbound with his magic.

Neel travelled over the whole world and was receptive to different cultures and preferences. Lina was open-minded and would often be fascinated by the stories Neel told her or the elements of different cultures he embraced according to his preferences.

Her life became easier.

But nobody ever knew……………….

Lina had a Prince of the Clouds who would love and look after her forever……………………..

❖ ❖ ❖